D0537796

This Little Tiger
book belongs to:

_____

_____

_____

_____

For my good friend Paeony Lewis
DB

For Heidi, Chloe and Ben
for their love, support and cups of tea
DH

LITTLE TIGER PRESS
An imprint of Magi Publications
1 The Coda Centre, 189 Munster Road, London SW6 6AW
www.littletigerpress.com
First published in Great Britain 2003
This edition published 2003
Text © David Bedford 2003
Illustration © Little Tiger Press 2003
David Bedford has asserted his right to be
identified as the author of this work under the
Copyright, Designs and Patents Act, 1988.
All rights reserved
ISBN 1 85430 860 2
A CIP catalogue record for this book is available from the British Library
Printed in Singapore
2 4 6 8 10 9 7 5 3

What Are You Doing in
My Bed?

David Bedford
illustrated by Daniel Howarth

LITTLE TIGER PRESS

London

Kip the kitten had nowhere to sleep
on a dark and cold winter's night.
So he crept through a door . . .

. . . and curled up warm and
snug in somebody's bed.

Then out of the dark
Kip heard . . .

. . . whispers and hisses,
and soft feet padding
through the night.

Bright green eyes peered
in through the window,
and suddenly . . .

. . . one, two, three, four, five, six cats
came banging through the cat door!
They tumbled and skidded and rolled
across the floor, where they found . . .

. . . Kip!
   "What are YOU doing in OUR bed?"
   shouted the six angry cats.

"Your bed?" said Kip.
"But this bed's too small for
you. You'd never all fit!"

"Never fit?" said the cats.
"Just you watch . . ."

One, two, three cats curled up
neatly, head to tail . . .

then four, five, six cats
piled on top.

"See? There's no room
  for you," they said.
"You'd never fit."

"Never fit?"
  said Kip.
"Just you
  watch . . ."

Tottering and teetering,
 Kip carefully climbed on top.
"I'll sleep here," he said.

"OK," the cats yawned.
"But don't fidget or snore."
 And they fell asleep in a heap.

 But suddenly, a big, deep,
 growly voice said . . .

"WHAT ARE YOU
DOING IN MY BED?
SCRAM!"

The cats skitter-skattered round the room, but only found hard, cold places to sleep.

Harry the dog was comfy in his bed,
and he soon began to snore.

But then an icy wind whistled in through
the cat door, and Harry awoke
and shivered.

Kip whispered, "Follow me . . ."
and he quickly led six cold cats
across the floor . . .

. . . to the cosy bed.
"We'll keep you warm,"
said Kip.

"You'll never all fit," chattered Harry.
"Never fit?" said Kip. "Just you watch . . ."

Kip and Harry snored right through the night under their warm blanket of cats.

And they all fitted purr-fectly!

Shaggy Dog and the Terrible Itch

David Bedford and Gwyneth Williamson

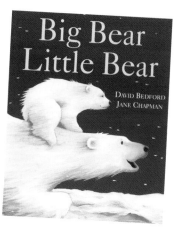
Big Bear Little Bear

DAVID BEDFORD
JANE CHAPMAN

Fidgety Fish

Ruth Galloway

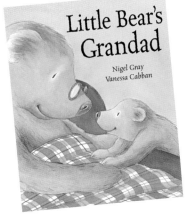
Little Bear's Grandad

Nigel Gray
Vanessa Cabban

More books to curl up with from Little Tiger Press

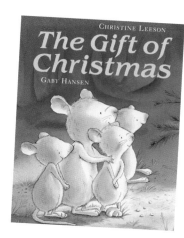
CHRISTINE LEESON
The Gift of Christmas

GABY HANSEN

Fireman PiggyWiggy

Christyan and Diane Fox

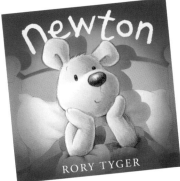
newton

RORY TYGER

For information regarding any of the above titles or for our catalogue, please contact us:
Little Tiger Press, 1 The Coda Centre, 189 Munster Road, London SW6 6AW
Tel: 020 7385 6333 Fax: 020 7385 7333 E-mail: info@littletiger.co.uk www.littletigerpress.com